AMISH LOST BABY

SWEET AMISH ROMANCE

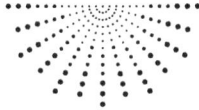

SARAH MILLER

SWEETBOOKHUB.COM

CHAPTER ONE

❧

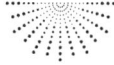

Worship the LORD your God,
and his blessing will be on your food and water.
I will take away sickness from among you,
Exodus 23:25

❧

Growing tired with sitting on the uncomfortable seat of the large bus, Suzanna Miller shifted her weight and rearranged the bundle of blankets that she held in her arms. Pushing a corner of the blue blanket aside, she peered down into the round, sleeping face of her tiny son. Warmth and love made her heart sing for just a moment.

The world outside the bus was dark and seemed evil; yet her son looked like an angel, nestled in her arms.

The only gut thing I have left, Suzanna thought to herself.

"Awww, he's precious!"

The crackling voice stunned Suzanna and made her jump in her seat. Turning, she looked over her shoulder and took notice of an elderly woman sitting behind her in the almost-empty bus. The old woman had a look of awe on her face as she studied the tiny boppli.

Suzanna pulled the bundle of blankets tighter against her chest. While the other passenger seemed harmless enough, she had learned one thing during her time in the *Englischer* world – no one was truly as innocent as they seemed.

Swallowing hard, Suzanna forced herself to sound at least half-way pleasant as she nodded her head and softly whispered, "*Denke* – thank you."

Leaning closer, the elderly woman continued to

study the boppli. "I'm traveling to see my new grandson. He was just born last night. How old is your little one?"

"Almost a month," Suzanna admitted. She felt a catch in her throat as memories of the boppli's birth assaulted her mind. It had been nothing like the joyful at-home births she was used to in her Amish community. Instead, it had been full of pain, agony, and a dull sense of loneliness as she gave birth in the sterile hospital room with no one at her side.

It's your own fault, Suzanna reminded herself quietly. She had been the one who had fallen for the ways of the *Englischer*, she had been the one who had chosen to turn her back on her family and her faith. She had been the one who had traded in everything for the chance of love with a man who only ended up using her before abandoning her. And now, Suzanna would be forced to bear the consequences of her actions for the rest of her life.

Peering down into the face of her sleeping son, she hated the thought that he would be forced to suffer along with her.

"What's his name?"

"It's David," Suzanna replied. She had named the boppli after her own *daed*. Sadly, Suzanna's *daed* would never get a chance to even meet his first grandchild.

He wouldn't want to anyway. Not considering all that had happened.

"Well," the elderly woman spoke up, "You're a mighty blessed woman. Both you and your husband."

With that, the other passenger leaned back against her seat, leaving Suzanna to her own thoughts.

Blessed. *Ach*, how could she ever hope to look at it that way? Suzanna felt cursed.

Closing her eyes, she let the last year of her life play through her mind. Suzanna could remember the first time that she saw David's father, Mike, hanging out at the grocery store. Despite the fact that she was an Amish teenager and he was a much older man of the world, the two of them seemed to have an instant connection. Suzanna could recall all the gut times that she and Mike had enjoyed, riding around in his red convertible and staying out late into the night.

When Mike had announced he was leaving Ohio to

become a musician in Nashville, TN, Suzanna had quickly agreed to go with him. Leaving a note for her parents, she ran off into the night.

It was supposed to be a fairy-tale, but it had quickly become a nightmare.

Mike had forced himself on her the first chance that he had, then left her alone on the street while he picked up another girl at a bar. The shame had been soul-crushing. What a fool she had been, and now she was alone.

Too ashamed to go home, she worked at a nearby motel cleaning rooms in exchange for a little pay and a place to spend the night. When she discovered she was pregnant, her heart broke once more. What had she done? Though having a little one had always been her dream, she never wanted to bring a kinner into the world like this!

Now that David was born, Suzanna realized how desperately she needed him to be raised in the Amish faith – a wish that seemed impossible if she was to keep him. There was no way she would be accepted back into the faith after all she had done.

Snuggling him tighter against her chest, she breathed in the fresh scent of her tiny son.

"I've got to do what's best for you, David," she whispered against his cute little ear, "I've got to do what's best!"

"Faith's Creek, one mile!" The bus driver called out over the bus's intercom system.

Gathering her courage, Suzanna prepared herself for whatever lay ahead in the unfamiliar Amish district. She could only hope that this trip would give both her and her son the new start they so desperately needed.

～

Every muscle in Suzanna's body ached as she made her way down the dusty road that stretched from Faith's Creek out into the country. It was almost daybreak, she must act fast before the Amish families rose for their early chores.

Shifting the weight of boppli David in her arms, Suzanna looked down into his sleeping face.

"Please, *Gott,*" she whispered the prayer into the

darkness and then looked up to scan the horizon for any Amish homes. "Please, *Gott*, let me find a place where David will be loved!" It was the first time that Suzanna had prayed since she ran away from her Amish home. She could only hope that the Lord would still listen to her after all that she had done.

Stopping beside a black mailbox, Suzanna leaned her weight against the top of it and squinted to read the letters on the side in the growing light of the day.

"Adam and Barbara Wengerd," Suzanna read the words aloud.

She let her eyes trail down the gravel lane that led toward an immaculate white clapboard house. It was a small home with no sign of any children's toys visible in the yard.

A home with no children.

Perhaps David would be the answer to this couple's prayers. Perhaps they had been pleading with the Lord for this little boppli for years.

Looking back at her sleeping infant, Suzanna felt a sob start to rise in her throat. How could she just leave him with strangers? And yet, how could she do any better?

Sucking in a deep breath, she started the long trek up the gravel lane, breathing endless silent prayers that she was making the right decision.

CHAPTER TWO

~

Hope deferred makes the heart sick,
but a longing fulfilled is a tree of life.
Proverbs 13:12

~

Adam Wengerd yawned as he reached for the kettle on the stove and proceeded to pour himself some coffee.

"You and that coffee!" His schweschder, Barbara, laughed as she walked past him with a shake of her head. "I'm fairly certain you keep the coffee companies in business."

Chuckling to himself, Adam gave a nod and replied, "*Ach*, Barbara, it's only my third cup today!"

Glancing out the window, he could see that the sun was already high above the barn, illuminating their farm.

Life hadn't turned out the way Adam had ever imagined. He had never dreamed that at twenty-five-years-old, he would still be living at the family farm with his older schweschder. But life had a strange way of throwing things in Adam's path that he hadn't planned. He guessed it made it interesting.

"I'd better go out and give the chickens their feed," he said as he made his way toward the door and reached for his black felt hat. "I think they're complaining more than usual this morning."

Stepping out into the warmth of the summer morning, Adam made his way toward the barn. If he wanted to get out and start chopping out the fields before it got blistering hot, he would need to hurry. Goodness knew that the hot Pennsylvania days could make it miserable to get his chores finished.

Heading directly into the barn, Adam went to the feed bin and measured out the amount of feed he would need for the chickens.

Their two dozen hens gave them enough eggs to support themselves and some to sell to their *Englischer* neighbors, helping Adam afford the feed bills.

Pulling the metal scooper out of the bin of rich corn, he thought he heard a strange noise. Standing up straighter, he cocked his head and listened more intently.

It was a soft whining sound – almost like a tiny muffled cry.

"I bet one of those crazy barn cats has managed to sneak off and have a litter of kittens!" Adam exclaimed aloud as he smiled softly. Although he had never considered himself to be a big fan of cats, there was nothing much cuter than a little fuzzy kitten.

Wahhh!!!

This time, the noise was more pronounced, and Adam realized it was no kitten.

"What in the world?" he asked himself as he hurried

toward the back of the barn and the unmistakable sound of a boppli in distress.

Stopping beside one of the dark and empty pens where the sheep were usually placed during lamb season, Adam could make out a bundle of blankets lying in a mound of hay.

The crying continued, urging Adam to rush into the pen and bend over to pick up the squirming blue blanket. Pushing a corner of the cover aside, he found himself staring into the perfectly round face of a beautiful boppli.

Forcing himself to breathe normally, Adam pulled himself to his feet.

"What are you doing here?" he asked, his voice sounding strange to his own ears. Why on earth would someone leave a boppli? Let alone leave it out here in the nasty old barn? Adam had to go show Barbara! Finding his strength, he sprinted toward the house, yelling out his schweschder's name the closer he got.

The front door swung open, and Barbara stepped out on the porch, her face turned down in a frown.

"*Ach*, Adam!" she exclaimed, "What are you yelling for?"

When her eyes traveled toward the bundle held in his arms, she let out a gasp and her hand flew to her throat.

"What are you doing with that?"

"It's a *boppli*, Barbara," Adam rushed to explain, pushing back the blankets to show her the round face of the fussing infant.

"I can see that," Barbara replied tartly, "But what are you doing with it? And where did it come from?"

Giving a shrug, Adam tried to get his mind to stop spinning so that he could explain what little he knew, "I just went out to the barn, and it was there in the blankets, placed back in one of the piles of hay in an empty pen."

Taking one of her long fingers, Barbara began to poke at the bundle almost as if she was scared of what was tucked inside.

"There's a note," she said as she worked to unpin a piece of paper from the edge of the blanket.

Adam held his breath as he watched his schweschder unfold the paper. He could only hope the note would give them some answers. Looking down into the sweet face of the kinner, he tried to understand why anyone would choose to leave their *boppli* in a place like that.

"This is David," Barbara began to read aloud, "He is a sweet little *boppli* boy who deserves a much better life than he has had. Because of his *mamm's* bad decisions, he has not got a family or a home. He needs to be raised by a loving couple who can teach him about *Gott* and the Amish faith. Perhaps *Gott* brought him to your home. Please take care of him."

Adam swallowed hard as the truth hit him. Someone had left this *boppli* as an act of love. Some poor *mamm* had tried to protect her kinner by finding a family to raise him. The thought of having to abandon a kinner to the care of strangers made Adam's heart ache.

Reaching a hand down into the blankets, he smiled softly when the *boppli* latched onto his finger.

"Well," Barbara huffed. "What do you make of that?"

"It's sad," Adam managed to mutter. "So sad to think of some poor *mamm* leaving her *boppli*." Looking up at his *schweschder*, he breathed the words that he hoped she would agree with, "I'm just glad that *Gott* saw fit to bring this little boy here – a home with no children and plenty of love to go around."

Ignoring his words entirely, Barbara motioned her *bruder* toward the house. "Let's get him inside and see if he needs his diaper changed. I never would have dreamed such a thing! It looks like I need to make a trip out to see Bishop Beiler. He might know who this *boppli* belongs to... maybe he can help this poor woman out so that she can keep this *kinner*."

Adam hoped the same thing, and yet, he couldn't stop a nagging feeling that this *boppli* was meant to be a part of his life forever. Although he had just met the little tyke, the idea of letting him go was already painful.

CHAPTER THREE

for everyone born of God overcomes the world.
This is the victory that has overcome the world,
even our faith.
John 5:4

T he tears that clouded her eyes made it hard for Suzanna to see the road in front of her as she made her way back toward Faith's Creek. She had nestled her son down in some hay in an empty stall and waited on the edge of the Wengerd property. Spying from a secluded spot beside a nearby tree line, she had watched when the owner of the barn discovered her David and rushed him to his house.

Even from a distance, Suzanna had been able to see that the Amish man cradling David in his arms was gentle and kind with her *boppli*. He would surely make David a *gut daed*.

"I did what was right for my son," Suzanna told herself as she pressed onward. She couldn't imagine what the future would hold for her now, but at least she knew that David would have a better life than anything she could offer. If only the pain and loneliness in her heart weren't so overwhelming!

The sound of horses' hooves clopping against the hard pavement of the road made Suzanna hurry to brush the tears off her face. If she had any hope of being accepted into this community, she couldn't let anyone know what she had just done!

"Hello there!" A cheerful voice called out from the approaching buggy.

Suzanna could tell that they were slowing their horses' walk even without turning her head.

Sucking in a deep breath, she gathered her courage and turned to look at the person sitting on the high buggy seat.

It was a lone Amish woman with a friendly smile across her weathered face. The older woman's brown eyes seemed trustworthy and caring as she studied Suzanna from her place on the wooden seat.

"*Gut* morning," she called out, "I don't think I've seen you around these parts before. Could you use a ride?"

Suzanna worked to regain her composure, hoping that no one could see that she had been crying. Tilting her head to one side, she considered her options – she could either accept this woman's invitation to ride in her buggy and perhaps gain a friend she desperately needed, or else she could continue to walk alone with no idea where to go.

Giving a nod, Suzanna stepped up to the side of the buggy and forced a smile. "*Jah*, that would be nice – *denke*."

Settling down on the buggy seat beside the older Amish woman, Suzanna found herself feeling strangely at ease.

"Where are you headed?"

The question took Suzanna by surprise, and she wasn't sure how to even answer. Giving a shrug, she whispered, "I'm not even sure, really." Although Suzanna had spent hours memorizing what she would say when the time came, the story now seemed trapped in her throat. "Somewhere that I can have a fresh start."

The other woman reached out to pat Suzanna on the hand as she said, "Then you've come to the right place! Faith's Creek is the perfect spot for new beginnings! What's your name, dear?"

Living in the harsh *Englischer* world, Suzanna had forgotten how it felt to be treated so kindly. Having someone speak to her softly made her feel like she might burst into tears.

"I'm Suzanna," she said.

"And I'm Sarah Beiler. My husband is Amos, the bishop here in the district." Giving Suzanna a knowing glance, she said, "You look like a girl who could use a gut cup of *kaffe* and some cinnamon buns. How about you come home with me until we can figure out where you're going next?"

The offer seemed like it could be the new beginning for which Suzanna had prayed. She nodded her head and gave a forced smile. She could only hope that she was making the right decision.

~

S itting in the kitchen at Bishop Beiler's home, Suzanna felt like she could hardly swallow the delicious cinnamon bun around the lump that was in her throat. While she was almost famished, all she could think about was her precious little boy – she missed David so much already! The idea of a future without him was almost more than she could bear.

Sarah pulled out a chair and sat across from Suzanna, a warm smile on her face as she picked up her cup of kaffe and took a long sip before speaking. "You seem so troubled, dear. What brought you to Faith's Creek?"

It was a question that Suzanna had expected, but it was still difficult to answer. Swallowing hard, she shrugged and tried to explain, "I'm from Ohio, but ended up leaving home for all the wrong reasons. I thought that the *Englischer* life was what I wanted, but it turned out I was wrong. I made many bad choices, and now I'm just trying to start over."

Looking up at Sarah's eyes, she was glad to see that the older woman seemed understanding. In the other room, Suzanna could see that Bishop Amos was silently rocking in his chair, allowing his wife the chance to talk. Even though she had just met them, her heart was warming toward the older couple. They seemed like they would have the compassion and ability to help Suzanna make her fresh start.

A knock on the door startled her, making her jump in her seat. She watched as Bishop Amos got up to see who had arrived. Swinging the door open, she could overhear him say, "*Gut* morning, Barbara! What brings you out this way?"

From her place at the table, Suzanna couldn't see the new guest, but she could overhear every word that was said.

"Sorry to bother you, Amos, but we've had something shocking happen at our home this morning. Adam went out to feed the animals, and he discovered a *boppli* hidden away in the barn!"

Suzanna felt her heart drop, and she couldn't breathe

normally as reality hit her. This woman was talking about little David!

"Give me a minute, dear," Sarah said as she stood up from her seat and went into the other room to join her husband.

Sitting alone in the kitchen, Suzanna listened intently as the new arrival explained about finding David in the barn. Just hearing the story retold made Suzanna feel like her heart would break in two. She wanted her son to grow up in the Amish faith with gut parents, but how could she stand to be apart from him?

"He's a sweet *boppli*," Barbara said. "But Adam and I know nothing about *kinner*. It only seems right that he should be with his real *mamm*. Bishop Amos, do you happen to have any idea who his *mamm* might be?"

Craning her neck so that she could see into the other room, Suzanna watched as the older man tugged at his white beard and shook his head. "No, I'm afraid not, but I will be looking into the matter. Until I can get some answers, would you and Adam be willing to give the *boppl*i a gut home? You're the only family that doesn't already have *kinner* of their own."

Suzanna held her breath until she heard the other woman say, "*Jah*, of course, we'll take care of him."

Sitting silently at the table, Suzanna thought about an old familiar childhood Bible story. This entire situation reminded her of Moses when he was found by the Pharaoh's daughter floating in a basket. In a strange twist of fate, Moses' own *mamm* had been hired to care for the *boppli,* allowing her the chance to spend time with Moses while her identity remained hidden.

An idea began to weave itself through Suzanna's mind. Maybe the Lord had provided her with the perfect way to be in her son's life, even though others would be considered his family!

CHAPTER FOUR

The LORD is with me;
I will not be afraid.
What can mere mortals do to me?
Psalm 118:6

C losing the door behind their departing
guest, Amos and Sarah Beiler looked at
each other with love and compassion.
What a day it had been! First, the appearance of a
strange and secretive Amish girl alongside the road,

and then Barbara Wengerd's shocking announcement about an abandoned *boppli*!

"Well," Amos said softly as he looked at his *fraa*, "What do you think of that news?"

Almost before the question was out of his mouth, they heard a noise from the kitchen doorway. Suzanna was standing there with an uncomfortable look on her face as she shifted her weight from one foot to another.

"I'm sorry, but I couldn't help overhearing all that," Suzanna said, "I think that it's so kind of that couple to take in a *boppli* that isn't their own, but they're taking on a mighty big responsibility. I have five younger siblings, so I know how difficult boppli's can be. I love *kinner* and would be happy to help them out while they have this kinner at their home... in exchange for room and board."

Sarah and Amos looked at each other once again, their minds practically spinning as they tried to understand why this newcomer to the community was making such an offer.

"I need a place to stay," she said as if she could instantly recognize their confusion, "and I want to help out. Maybe this is the best way for me to get involved in the district and become a part of the faith again."

Sarah started to open her mouth, but Amos spoke up before she could say a word, "Suzanna, we appreciate your offer, but you just got here and are tired. We can talk it over more tonight and see how you feel about it in the morning. If you still want to help then, we can go out to the Wengerd's place and make the offer."

The first smile crossed Suzanna's lips, and she nodded. "*Jah*, that sounds *gut!*"

~

Adam Wengerd let out a deep sigh as he repositioned the crying *boppli* in his arms. Looking down into the squealing face of the infant, it was hard to imagine how a *kinner* so small could make so much noise! He had been up most of the night trying to care for the little *boppli*. Although Barbara was a gut *schweschder* and housekeeper, she didn't seem interested in helping with childcare – she had never had much of a way with *kinner*.

Using his free hand to pour himself a cup of *kaffe*, Adam let out a sharp yell when he accidentally poured some of the hot liquid on his socked foot.

A knock on the door made him jump again, and he almost spilled some more.

Barbara appeared from a backroom, a disgruntled look on her face as she made her way to the door. Swinging it open, she revealed Sarah Beiler standing beside an unfamiliar young Amish woman.

"Come in," Barbara said as she ushered the guests into their home. "I'm sorry things are a mess, but life has been a little upside down since the arrival of the *boppli*."

Letting his eyes travel toward the stranger, Adam felt himself blushing when he thought of how out of sorts he must look. Standing there with a screaming *boppli* in his arms, Adam realized that his clothes were wrinkled, and his hair hadn't even been combed.

"I think I may have a solution to your problems," Sarah said as she nodded her head toward the stranger. "This is Suzanna. She is new in the community and looking for some work. When she heard about your situation, she offered to come to help you out with the *boppli*."

Glancing toward his *schweschder*, Adam could see Barbara instantly bristle.

Before she could say a word, Suzanna stepped toward Adam and held out her arms. "Could I try to calm him down?"

Nodding, Adam handed the *boppli* toward the pretty young woman.

"Hush now, little one," Suzanna said as she looked lovingly into the face of the infant and started to softly sway back and forth. Almost as if by magic, David instantly stopped crying.

"Well, I'll be!" Adam said with a shake of his head. He couldn't help but think how beautiful this gentle Amish girl looked as she held the abandoned *kinner* against her chest, "It sure looks like you have a way with *boppli's*!"

"I do. I will happily stay here and take care of the *boppli* if you'll just let me have a place to live and food to eat."

"I'm just not sure about this," Barbara said, her voice betraying her uncertainty.

Grabbing his *schweschder* by the arm, Adam led her toward the corner of the room and lowered his voice. "Barbara, we agreed to take care of this *kinner* until his *mamm* can be found, but it's going to kill us both if we don't get some sleep." Glancing back toward Suzanna, he smiled when he saw the tender looks she was giving David. "This girl is almost like a miracle! And you know that Sarah and Amos wouldn't send someone our way if they weren't sure that it was a gut idea."

Giving a shrug, Barbara finally relented. "I suppose you're probably right."

Suzanna would be staying with them, and Adam found himself excited about not only getting a night of sleep but also the chance to get to know this strange girl.

CHAPTER FIVE

To the roots of the mountains I sank down;
the earth beneath barred me in forever.
But you, LORD my God, brought my life up from
the pit.
Jonah 2:6

Lying in the small twin bed, Suzanna smiled to herself as she opened her eyes and soaked in the morning sunlight streaming through the window. The guest room in the Wengerd's house already felt like home to her, and she was glad to have a place to call her own.

Looking toward the foot of her bed, she could see the form of David sleeping soundly in his bassinet.

She had now been living with the Wengerds for almost two weeks, and it still felt like a dream. This was the happiest that she had been since she first met David's father and chose to leave the Amish faith. Perhaps *Gott* had truly seen fit to give her a second chance.

Forcing herself out of bed, Suzanna hurried to get dressed so that she could start her daily chores. She needed to see if she could help around the house some before David awoke.

Tiptoeing into the kitchen, she found Barbara already standing by the stove, preparing to fix some homemade muffins.

"*Gut* morning," Suzanna said. It felt like she had to force the words out of her mouth. While she appreciated that Barbara had willingly opened her home to David, it was easy to tell that she was not happy to have Suzanna there.

Barbara simply gave a nod before saying, "I'm about to run into town to talk to Bishop Amos to see if he's learned anything about David's *mamm*. I have other errands to run as well, so I'll likely be gone until this afternoon. Adam will be home if you need anything. Can you get these muffins out of the oven when they're done?"

Suzanna felt a knot in her stomach as she nodded her head. Every day she lived in fear that she would be found out. That Barbara would somehow discover that she was David's *mamm*.

Seeing Barbara out the door, Suzanna was glad to have the other woman leave. She could only hope that Adam would also stay out of the house, giving her the chance to gather her thoughts in private.

She let herself melt into one of the rocking chairs in the empty house. Closing her eyes, she said a soft prayer, "*Gott*, I hope that I'm doing the right thing here. I hope that it truly was You that brought me to the home of this couple and planned for them to be David's new family. Please, don't let Barbara discover the truth."

Suzanna had just breathed the last words of her

prayer when the front door swung open, and a smiling Adam stepped into the house. He looked almost surprised when he caught sight of Suzanna sitting in the rocking chair, and he chuckled as he said, "Oh, I'm sorry! I hope I didn't scare you. I just thought I would come back in for some *kaffe*. As Barbara says, I just can't seem to get enough of it."

Feeling like it was her duty to serve, Suzanna tried to find her footing. "I can get it…"

"No," Adam cut her short and raised his hand. "You've got to be tired from taking care of little David. You get some rest. How about I fix you a cup too?"

It felt uncomfortable to have a man waiting on her, but she found herself nodding her head in agreement. "*Jah* – that would be nice. *Denke.*"

Watching Adam bustle around the stove, working to prepare the warm drink, Suzanna felt a pang of sadness stab through her heart. He was a gut, honest man who obviously cared about Barbara. If Suzanna had stayed in her community and had never wandered off after an *Englischer* man, perhaps she could have had a husband just as tender and kind.

"Here you go," Adam said as he came to her side and extended a cup of the warm *kaffe*.

Smiling her thanks, Suzanna took the extended cup and took a drink.

To her surprise and dread, Adam took the rocking chair directly across from her. Watching him drink his own *kaffe*, Suzanna had to force herself to breathe normally. During her time with the Wengerds, she had tried to stay out of their way and avoid the chance to be alone with either of them. What if he began to ask her questions about her past?

"*Denke* for all that you're doing for David," Adam said as he looked up from his drink and studied Suzanna. "We truly do appreciate it."

His gaze seemed so tender and almost attractive that it made Suzanna turn away. Studying her hands, she tried to shrug as she said, "I've been happy to do it."

"You truly do have a way with *kinner*," he continued as he took another sip from his cup. "Didn't you say that you have a lot of siblings?"

Trying to shrug off his questions, she smiled. "Don't most Amish have a lot of siblings?"

Her comment caused Adam to chuckle, and she could only hope that he would decide to go back outside to work.

"How old are you, Suzanna? You seem young to be out on your own."

Feeling a blush start to rise to her cheeks, she thought about all that she had endured in the last year. It was hard to imagine that she still looked young. "I'm eighteen."

Scooting his chair closer to hers, Adam stared intently into her eyes. "How did you end up out here in the world all by yourself?"

Suzanna hated his questions. Not only did they make her uncomfortable, but they also brought to mind a thousand unpleasant memories. Just considering all that had happened to tear her away from her family made her feel like she might burst into tears. Biting down on her lip, she tried to still her nerves.

"I'm sorry," Adam said quickly, obviously noticing her concern. "I shouldn't have asked so much..."

He sounded so sincere and genuinely caring that she

found herself shaking her head. "No, don't be sorry. Of course, you have questions about me – I'm a stranger living in your house! I just..." Suzanna's voice trailed off as she grappled for the right words. "The past has been painful, and I don't like to think about it."

Tears began to well up in her eyes, and she had to fight to keep her emotions in control. Closing her eyes, she began to breathe a prayer of help, begging the Lord to calm her nerves and make it possible for her to maintain her composure.

A firm, calloused hand covered hers, instantly filling Suzanna's entire body with a comforting warmth. Opening her eyes, she looked directly into Adam's kind and handsome face. The young man had scooted closer and had clasped onto her hand. As he gazed into her face, it seemed almost as if he could see into her very soul.

What am I doing? Suzanna asked herself. How could she be allowing herself to feel so much tenderness for another woman's husband? Jerking her hand away, she forced herself to grow firm.

"I'd like to ask you to keep your hands to yourself!"

Her words were hot as she almost spat them out in Adam's direction.

Instant shame filled the young man's face, and he sputtered as he tried to explain, "I'm sorry. I didn't mean..."

Suzanna didn't give him the chance to get out any type of excuse. Standing up, she crossed her arms firmly against her chest and jutted out her bottom jaw. "What kind of a man clasps the hand of an unmarried woman as soon as his *fraa* leaves home? I would have thought better of you, Adam Wengerd!"

Perhaps she had made a terrible mistake leaving her *boppli* with this couple! She didn't want David raised by a man who would act in such a way.

Adam's eyes grew large, and he cocked his head to one side. It appeared that he was completely speechless and confused. "My *fraa*?"

"*Jah*, your *fraa*! Barbara's only been gone a few minutes, surely you haven't forgotten about her already!"

Recognition suddenly crossed Adam's face, and he let out an unexpected chuckle. Shaking his head, a smile began to play at the corners of his lips. "You mean Barbara?" he asked with merriment in his eyes. "Barbara is not my *fraa*!"

Now it was Suzanna's turn to be confused. She stepped back and knit her brows together, wondering how he could expect to trick her with such a ridiculous statement.

"If she's not your *fraa*, then what is she?"

Reaching up to rub his hand against his face, Adam shook his head. "Barbara is my *schweschder*."

His *schweschder*? It seemed almost impossible to believe, and yet, as Suzanna considered the days that she had spent in the Wengerd home, the more possible it became. No wonder the couple hadn't seemed very affectionate with one another!

"Your *schweschder*," Suzanna said, it was almost more of a whisper than a statement. Her face grew warm again as she looked up to meet Adam's gaze, "Goodness, what a fool I've been."

"Please, sit," Adam directed back toward the chair. "Finish your *kaffe* and talk some more with me."

Obeying his suggestion, she sat down and tried to make sense of the new information.

"Barbara is my unmarried *schweschder*," Adam said with a twinkle in his eye. "I should have explained that from the start, but I just thought that it was obvious."

"I am so sorry..."

Putting up a hand, Adam stopped her. "No need to be sorry. I guess it makes sense that we would seem like a married couple to someone who doesn't know our situation."

Looking down at her hands, Suzanna folded them in her lap and smiled softly. "It did seem that way." Trying to collect her thoughts, she asked, "So, you're not married?"

He was smiling when she looked back up at him. "No. I'm not married." Reaching for his cup of *kaffe*, Adam took another sip before explaining, "A few years ago, I was to be married... but that all fell apart. Her name was Rosy. She got sick and... I lost her."

It was easy to hear the pain in his voice.

"After that, I just gave up all my hopes of ever having

a *fraa* or a family. I got used to just living here with Barbara until…"

His words trailed off and, while Suzanna didn't want to pry, she could hardly stop herself. Looking up to meet his gaze, she asked, "Until what?"

Smiling softly, he said, "Until David came along."

Leaning back in the hard-rocking chair, Suzanna studied Adam as he drank down the last of his *kaffe*. He was truly a handsome man, and it seemed his heart was even bigger than she had imagined possible.

The Lord surely had brought David to this man. And, for a moment, Suzanna hoped that *Gott* had brought her to Adam as well.

CHAPTER SIX

❧

*For the foolishness of God is wiser than human
wisdom, and the weakness of God is stronger than
human strength.*
1 Corinthians 1:25

❧

Standing inside the barn, Adam lifted the
pitchfork and brought it down into the dirty
straw before giving it a firm toss into the
empty wheelbarrow. Try as he might to think about
other things, it seemed that Suzanna was the only
thing on his mind these days. It was no secret to

Adam that he was beginning to have feelings for the strange young woman who had found her way into his life.

"Can we talk?"

The question made Adam jump, and he turned to see his *schweschder* standing behind him. Barbara had a frown on her face as she crossed her arms against her chest.

"*Jah*, of course."

Barbara stepped up closer, her expression betraying that something was bothering her.

"Adam," she said, "It's starting to feel like that *boppli* just dropped out of thin air. No matter who I talk to, no one seems to have an idea who his *mamm* might be."

Wiping his forehead against his shirt sleeve, Adam felt a sense of relief that she hadn't found out anything about David's parents. He was growing to love the boy more with each day and wanted to keep the *kinner* for himself. "It's starting to just seem like *Gott* placed that *boppli* in our lives, Barbara. Perhaps He knew that we needed a boppli."

Barbara raised a critical eyebrow. "*Gott* doesn't just drop *boppli's* out of heaven, *bruder*. And he doesn't drop women, either."

Her words made Adam's heart start to race. "I don't know what you mean."

Ignoring his feigned innocence, Barbara stepped up closer to him and said, "I'm not blind. I see the way that you and that strange girl look at each other. She's got a past... and, as hard as she tries to hide it, I'd dare say it's a dark one. Be wary of her. She's probably not what she seems."

Turning on her heel, Barbara left the barn behind and started toward the house, marching almost like a soldier.

Letting out a deep breath, Adam tried to brush her warning aside. His *schweschder* had always been one to be too cautious and make too much out of a situation.

Looking up, Adam felt a sense of lightness return to his heart when he saw Suzanna walking through the yard, *boppli* David held tightly against her hip. She was obviously pointing things out to him, whispering words against his face, likely telling the tiny *kinner* secrets. Even though he was too young to speak or even seem to understand, she obviously wanted to share things with him.

"She makes a gut *mamm* for him," Adam said to himself.

Suddenly feeling bold, Adam tossed his pitchfork aside and stepped out of the barn. Making his way to Suzanna's side, he said, "I see that you're out enjoying the fine weather! Would you like to see the rest of the farm? Maybe take a walk with me down by the pond?"

For a moment, a look of confusion and fear seemed to cross the beautiful young woman's eyes, but, just as quickly, it was replaced by something else. Smiling ever so slightly, she nodded her head. "*Jah*, that would be wonderful."

Leading Suzanna toward the pond with David held tightly against her, Adam allowed himself to soak in the happy feelings that were playing in his heart. When he was with Suzanna and David, it seemed like everything was right in the world. He hated to even think of what his life would be like if this young Amish woman ever decided to leave them.

"Here's the pond," Adam said, forcing his mind away from the terrible thought and back to reality. Picking up a smooth stone, he pulled back his hand and then released it, sending the rock skipping across the water.

Looking toward Suzanna, he smiled. "Did you ever skip rocks when you were a little girl?"

Nodding her head, she assured him that she had. "Oh yes – and I was known for being quite gut at it."

"Here," Adam said, stepping up close to her. "I'll hold David, and you show me how *gut* you really are."

There was a twinkle in Suzanna's eyes as she accepted the challenge. She handed the *boppli* to Adam and then picked up a smooth rock from the water's edge. As she pulled her arm back and let go of the rock, Adam realized that his eyes were more firmly planted on her than on the stone that made its way across the pond.

"How was that for a toss?" her voice sounded merrier than ever as the stone made a splashing noise and sent small waves up behind it.

Pretending that he had been paying attention, he nodded his head. "I guess you are quite the expert."

"I should be," Suzanna said as she bent down to pick up another stone. "I used to spend hours skipping rocks with my *bruder*."

"How long has it been since you talked to your *bruder*?" The question slipped from Adam's lips before he could stop it. Seeing a shadow of sadness cross Suzanna's beautiful face, he instantly wished that he had kept his nosey questions to himself.

"Too long," she said with a voice that was little more than a whisper. She sent another rock sailing through the air, but this one landed with a *thunk* against the top of the water and instantly sunk.

Trying to lighten the mood, Adam shifted the weight of David in his arms and began to make cooing noises toward the tiny boy.

"He sure is growing! It's amazing how fast time goes by when you have a *boppli* in the house." Adam said. "I remember before you two came, some days felt like they would drag on forever. Now, no days seem long enough. I just want to savor them all."

Stepping up to his side, Suzanna peered over Adam's arm so that she could see David. "He is certainly a precious one."

With Suzanna standing so close, Adam could almost smell the soft fragrance of her hair, and he had to stop himself from becoming completely addlebrained.

"You're mighty *gut* with him," Adam said, watching the young woman closely as she reached out to take David into her own arms. "I had never realized what a huge responsibility a *boppli* could be. You've done better than any other nurse ever could!"

As she cradled David against her chest, Adam allowed himself to speak words that he had long kept deep inside. "I had always wanted to have a family of my own. It had just seemed so unlikely after everything that happened. When Rosy died, I thought that all my hopes of a future had died with her."

A sad smile crossed Suzanna's lips. "I had always wanted a family, too. As a little girl, my dream was to have a husband and some *kinner*. More than anything in the world, I just wanted to be loved and

47

feel safe." Her voice darkened as she admitted, "But I did a gut job messing all that up. I decided to run off after a wild lifestyle and threw it all away. In the end, my choices were nothing but sinful and hollow."

Such a sadness seemed to overtake her that Adam wished he could simply gather her in his arms and pull her close against his chest. How could a young woman with so much to offer, feel like her life was over?

Perhaps it was time that he and Suzanna both had a chance to experience a different way of life. Maybe the Lord had brought them together to show them each that there was still a chance for them to have what they most desperately wanted.

Reaching for another smooth stone, Adam let it roll around in his hands absentmindedly. Maybe there was a chance that he and Suzanna could still make one another's long lost dreams come true.

CHAPTER SEVEN

❧

"Go, stand in the temple courts," he said,
"and tell the people all about this new life."
Acts 5:20

❧

Shifting her weight back and forth, Suzanna enjoyed the feel of the hard rocking chair beneath her body as she rocked David to sleep. She knew that Adam himself had made the chair expressly for her to use for the *boppli*. The longer she stayed at the Wengerd home, the more she began to feel like she belonged.

But you don't belong, Suzanna reminded herself. No matter how much she might want to be a part of this family, she was nothing more than a girl that they were providing shelter in exchange for taking care of her own son! What would ultimately happen to her? She could hardly stand the idea of moving on without the Wengerds... especially moving on without David and Adam. The Amish man had become so important to her during the time that they had spent together.

Pulling herself to her feet, she peered into the sleeping face of her son and craned her neck to kiss one of his soft cheeks. He was growing so quickly that she wanted to savor every moment. She gently placed him into his bassinet, careful not to wake him.

Standing up straighter, she rubbed her back and decided that it was the perfect time to step outside for some fresh air. There was nothing like the peaceful country sounds of the night to soothe her troubled thoughts.

Tiptoeing outside, she pulled the squeaky door shut behind her and made her way to the edge of the porch. She looked up at the night sky and then closed her eyes, soaking in her surroundings.

"Please, *Gott*," she said softly. "Let it stay this way forever."

"Suzanna?"

The voice of Adam made her jump, and her eyes flew open. She could make out the form of the handsome young man returning from some work out in the barn. The closer he drew to the house, the harder Suzanna's heart beat within her chest.

"What are you doing out here?" Adam asked, a smile obvious on his handsome face.

Shrugging her shoulders, she explained, "Sometimes it's gut to be able to get away and just think for a while."

Making his way up the porch steps, Adam approached her side and leaned his elbows against the porch railing. "I suppose we both have plenty to be thinking about these days."

Suzanna raised an eyebrow, trying to make sense of his words. At this moment, all she could focus on were the butterflies fluttering in her stomach. Although she and Adam spent a lot of time together, most of it involved doing things with David or Barbara – rarely were they ever alone.

"What do you think about?" Adam asked.

Although Suzanna usually hated such intrusive questions, a part of her wanted to answer him. She wished that there didn't have to be so many secrets between the two of them. Sucking in a deep breath of air, she leaned her own weight against the railing, her shoulder almost touching his as she admitted the truth. "I'm thinking about the future – wondering what it might possibly hold for me."

Adam was silent for a moment until his husky voice said, "I've been wondering the same thing."

To Suzanna's complete surprise, he slid his hand across the railing and put it over hers, cupping her hand tenderly within his. Looking at their intertwined fingers, she felt an urge to be completely engulfed by this kind, good-hearted man.

"I'm never a bold man, Suzanna," Adam said as he turned to look in her eyes. "I'm not *gut* with women – which is probably one reason that I never found the strength to move on after Rosy. But seeing you...

getting to know you... it's been enough to give me courage."

With each word that he spoke, Suzanna felt her heart beat a little faster. Everything seemed so much like a dream that she was afraid that she might wake up at any minute.

"During the time that we've spent together, I've watched how gut you are with David. I've seen the way that you care for him. You've proven yourself to be a sweet, caring, and loving woman. I don't know what will happen with David, but I know that I don't want to lose you. You are exactly the type of woman that I want to spend the rest of my life with."

Tears began to gather in Suzanna's eyes as she soaked up the words that he was saying. With each second that passed, she grew deeper and deeper in love with the man standing at her side.

"Suzanna, will you please let me love you for as long as we both live?" Adam asked, "Will you please be my *fraa*?"

The question was so overwhelming that she could hardly accept it as the truth. Closing her eyes, she tried to believe that this was really happening. Could Suzanna truly have a chance at happiness?

Obviously, taking her silence as a refusal, Adam began to stutter as he said, "If you don't want to, I do understand…"

Turning her hand over, Suzanna clasped tighter to his as she said, "Adam, I have made some terrible mistakes during my teenage years. I have been so lost and have felt like I had no future. But being with you, coming to Faith's Creek, and being able to spend time with you, has reminded me that my life isn't over. Here I feel like I do have a chance at a home." Sucking in a deep breath of air, she said the words that Suzanna had never expected to utter, "Adam Wengerd, I would be honored to get to spend the rest of my life by your side. There is nothing that could make me any happier."

Tears were blurring Suzanna's vision, but she couldn't mistake the complete joy that overwhelmed the man in front of her. Reaching out, he wrapped his arms around her, pulling her into a warm embrace.

Nestled against Adam's chest, Suzanna felt like she

was finally where she was meant to be. For the first time in her life, she was safe and protected with a man that truly loved her.

What would he do if he knew all that you have done? A voice seemed to tease the back of Suzanna's mind. *Would he still love you then?* Shaking her head, she forced the thoughts to leave her alone. It didn't matter what would happen, because Adam never had to know. *Gott* had obviously brought them together – now she would just have to trust that He would protect her many dark secrets.

CHAPTER EIGHT

So then, just as you received Christ Jesus as Lord,
continue to live your lives in him,
7 rooted and built up in him,
strengthened in the faith as you were taught,
and overflowing with thankfulness.
Colossians 2:6-7

O pening his eyes, Adam blinked and then smiled to himself. Sunlight was already streaming in through the windows, alerting him that he had slept in for much too long.

After all the excitement of the previous night, he had found it difficult to ever go to sleep.

Suzanna had agreed to be his *fraa*. Even now, it seemed impossible to believe that it was true. Finally, all of Adam's dreams were going to be realized. He would have the beautiful young Amish woman as his *fraa,* and they could give *boppli* David the home that he deserved.

Pulling himself to his feet, Adam hurried to get dressed. He would need to take Suzanna to talk with Bishop Amos so that they could make plans for the announcement and set a time for the upcoming wedding.

"Denke, *Gott*," Adam said his prayer as little more than a whisper, "*Denke* for finally giving me some happiness in my life!"

Pulling on his black shoes, Adam went into the kitchen where his *schweschder* was washing some dishes by the sink. He let his gaze sweep over the empty room, looking for Suzanna.

"She's not here," Barbara said, almost as if she could read his mind.

Unable to hide the grin on his face, Adam went to his *schweschder's* side and reached for an empty cup.

"Suzanna's out in the yard with David," Barbara didn't even take a breath before asking, "Why did you sleep in so late today?"

Filling his cup up with hot *kaffe*, Adam shrugged and tried to decide just how much he should tell her. It was no secret that Barbara didn't like Suzanna, but he knew that she would need to know about the engagement eventually. "Barbara, I know this is going to come as somewhat of a surprise, but I have got news for you. Last night, I asked Suzanna to be my *fraa*."

Instantly, his *schweschder* bristled. She turned the dishrag in her hands nervously, her eyebrows raised in cold shock.

"I know she's not a friend of yours yet," Adam said. "But I am sure that you and Suzanna will learn to love each other with time. She is so *gut* with David and just seems to fit in here." Feeling a surge of joy as he considered the upcoming marriage, he said, "And she makes me happy. For the first time since Rosy died, I feel truly happy."

Turning on her heel, Barbara faced Adam. She seemed to brace herself before opening her mouth to say, "Adam, I wish I could tell you that I'm happy for you, but I'm not."

The words were so blunt that Adam almost felt like he could fall over from the impact.

"This girl is not who she claims to be."

"What are you talking about?" Even as he asked the question, Adam began to worry that he wouldn't want to know the answer. His *schweschder* wasn't one to try to give him a warning without a *gut* reason.

Closing her eyes, Barbara took in a deep breath. "I got a letter yesterday from one of our cousins in Ohio. She said that they had a girl in their community named Suzanna Miller. She was a wild teenager who took things a bit too far in her *rumspringa*. This Suzanna ran off with an *Englischer* and threw all her Amish ways behind."

The words were difficult for Adam to hear, but they weren't totally shocking. "Suzanna has told me that she made mistakes..."

Interrupting her *bruder*, Barbara put a steadying

59

hand on his arm. "Word has it that Suzanna became pregnant and gave birth to a *boppli* boy."

Adam felt like the life had been kicked right out of him. What was his *schweschder* saying?

As if she knew that she would have to spell it out for him, Barbara said, "I guess it's no wonder that she's so gut with *boppli* David. It certainly seems like she's his real *mamm*."

His real *mamm*. How could this be true? Did this mean that Suzanna had been fooling them all along? When she had pretended to be so helpful with David, was it just a plot to get to spend time with a *kinner* that was actually hers?

"She's pulled the wool over all our eyes," Barbara said softly.

Wishing that he could be sure that it was just a lie, Adam groaned and reached up to rub his hand against his forehead.

The front door swung open abruptly, and Suzanna came practically skipping inside with David held against her hip. She was smiling cheerfully, almost as light and airy as if she was a little bird.

Looking at her, Adam felt like a knife had been stabbed deep into his chest. Could it really be true? Could this woman that he had grown to love actually be a deceiver?

"*Gut* morning!" she said, her eyes sparkling as she planted a kiss on the top of David's head. "I had wondered when you were going to be up!"

Assailed by a thousand different questions, Adam forced himself to stand up straighter and look her in the eye. "Suzanna, we need to talk."

Instantly, her expression grew dark. She studied Adam as if he had become the enemy standing right in front of her. All the love that had been in her eyes moments earlier seemed to disappear, and Adam wondered if his fiancé would turn and run in the other direction.

"We've had news from Ohio, Suzanna," Barbara said with a voice that seemed cold and unfeeling. "We learned about your past, and we now know the truth."

Suzanna's eyes got large, and Adam could instantly see that everything he feared was the truth. Any hope he held that his fiancé was innocent was quickly wiped from his mind. A thousand terrible thoughts assaulted him at once.

How could Suzanna have done such a thing? It made Adam question all that he knew about the girl he was supposed to marry. Her love for David had been one of the things that had drawn Adam to her. Now, he found himself wondering what kind of woman would just abandon their *boppli* in a barn stall to be discovered by strangers. Perhaps Suzanna was not the caring, kind woman that he had believed.

Standing in front of them, Suzanna looked like a scared animal. Her chest began to rise and fall quickly beneath her simple blue dress, and her eyes searched the room for an escape.

"How could you?" Adam asked, his voice harsher than he had even intended, "How could you have tricked us like this?"

"This was all part of your plan all along, wasn't it?" Barbara jumped in to suggest, her tone more reprimanding than even that of Adam. "You meant to deceive us from the start! You tried to worm your way into our lives and into my *bruder's* affections!"

Tears were starting to gather in Suzanna's eyes, and

her body was shaking. Almost as if he sensed her upset, David began to cry. Adam felt so betrayed that he thought he might cry as well. At any other time, Adam would have wanted to rush to Suzanna's side and comfort her, but now everything had changed.

"I didn't!" Suzanna said her tone firm as she reached up to wipe at her eyes. "I had never meant to trick anyone. I only wanted David to have a gut life."

So, she even admitted what she had done. She didn't try to formulate a lie or explain it all away. Unable to hold back his comments any longer, Adam asked, "How could you do such a thing to David? How could you just abandon him in a stranger's barn?"

Swallowing hard, Suzanna tried to quiet the crying *boppli* before saying, "I knew that anywhere would be better than what I could give him. I thought that maybe *Gott* had brought me here..."

Barbara let out an incredulous snort and put a hand on her hip. "Let's not bring the Lord into this! You obviously played us and pretended to have feelings for my *bruder* simply so that you could secure a place to live."

Spoken aloud, the words hurt much more than

Adam could have ever imagined. It felt like he had been stabbed in the chest with a knife. His *schweschder's* statements were likely true – Suzanna had never loved him, she had just pretended to so that she wouldn't be homeless.

"Adam," Suzanna stepped forward and put a hand on his arm, her voice pleading him to trust her. "You can't believe that's true! I would never lie about my feelings for you. You mean so much to me..."

The lies were more than Adam could stand to hear. He pulled back his arm and lowered his gaze, unwilling to even look at the girl who had used him so cruelly.

Turning, Adam pushed past both his *schweschder* and his ex-fiancé. He had to get out of the house and have a chance to collect his thoughts.

❧

Watching Adam storm out of the house, Suzanna felt like her heart might break in two. She loved him so much, and yet she had hurt him so badly! It seemed like there was no way for her to convince him that she truly cared for him.

Reaching up to rub a frustrated hand across her face, she realized that her chances of happiness had slipped through her fingers. Once again, it seemed like her past mistakes would follow her for the rest of her life. She had to get away. There was no reason for her to stay.

"I hope you're happy!" Barbara's harsh voice snapped, making Suzanna feel like yet another knife had been sent through her heart.

A whimpering noise from David reminded her that she still had someone to think about. No matter what had happened between her and the Wengerds, David didn't deserve to pay for her bad choices. Adam and Barbara loved the little boy – he had the best chance at a happy life living with them.

"Here," Suzanna stepped up and placed the *boppli* into Barbara's arms. "Please, take care of him."

Before the other woman could say a word, Suzanna turned on her heel and made a break for the door. She didn't know where she would go, but she knew that she had to get away from the Wengerd's and the pain that she had brought on the kind siblings.

CHAPTER NINE

*Therefore confess your sins to each other and pray for
each other so that you may be healed.
The prayer of a righteous person is powerful and
effective.*
James 5:16

Sarah Beiler poured flour onto her kitchen
counter and began to run her weathered
hands across it before reaching for the bowl
of dough that she had placed on the stove.

"Something smells *gut*," Amos said as he stepped up behind her and tried to peer around her shoulder at what she was doing.

Playfully slapping him with a flour-covered hand, Sarah laughed and said, "Hard for my sticky buns to smell very gut when they haven't even been in the oven yet!"

Glancing back at her husband, Sarah saw him grin and give a shrug. "I can't help it. I'm so used to your food that I can smell it before it even starts baking."

Sarah started to give a comment of her own but stopped short when she heard a strange noise. Cocking her head to one side, she raised a hand to silence her husband. "Do you hear that? It sounds like someone crying."

His face crinkled in confusion as Amos listened with her. Unwilling to wait any longer, Sarah hurried to the back door and pulled it open, stepping out into the fresh sunshine of the noonday. She almost fell over the form of a young Amish woman, crouched over on their porch.

"Suzanna?" Sarah asked as she reached down and

placed a gentle hand on the top of the girl's prayer *kapp*. "Child, what is wrong?"

Suzanna looked up with eyes that were stained with tears. "I've made a bad mistake. Please, I need some help."

Hurrying the young woman into their house, Sarah and Amos led her to the large dining room table. Although they had only known the girl for a short period of time, the couple had quickly grown to care for her. They had hoped that she had a gut future ahead of her in their community. Seeing her in so much pain hurt them deeply.

While the sticky buns were long forgotten, Sarah got some *kaffe* and cake to give their guest. Usually, these treats were just what troubled souls needed to calm their spirits and become relaxed enough to speak their problems aloud.

"Suzanna... tell us what happened."

At first, the girl told the story with some difficulty, her words coming slowly as she tried to recall the mistakes that she had made in her wild *rumspringa*. She told about the way that she had fallen for David's father and how the evil man had misused her. The longer she talked, the more comfortable she became.

"I never meant to misuse Adam or Barbara," Suzanna said as she finished her story. "I had honestly hoped that the Lord was bringing me to a fresh start as Adam's *fraa*. I had thought he would never know about my past. Now, I've hurt him so badly..." Her voice trailed off, and it was easy to see that she was heartbroken to have caused him such pain.

Sitting up straighter in his chair, Amos cleared his throat. "Suzanna, we have all made mistakes in our past. While some of our sins may not have had such obvious consequences, no one human is perfect. That's why *Gott* has offered us the gift of forgiveness through His Son, Jesus Christ. If you have been forgiven by the Lord, then there is no reason to be ashamed or try to hide your past... He is the only one with the right to judge, and He deems us forgiven as soon as we ask."

Looking down at her hands, Suzanna's eyes filled with tears once again. "I want to believe the words that you say, but it's so difficult. I have never truly felt like the Lord forgave me for the wrongs that I have done, and I've never really asked him."

Overcome with compassion, Sarah placed a weathered hand over Suzanna's. "Then why don't we change all that right now?"

Through the tears that were streaming down her cheeks, Suzanna nodded her head. Although her heart was still broken over all that had happened with Adam and the fear of losing her son, she bowed her head and asked the Lord to forgive her for all the wrongs that she had done. With the Bishop and his *fraa* at her side, Suzanna recognized that *Gott* was the only one who could make all things right.

∽

Wiping some sweat from his brow, Adam rearranged the makeshift *boppli* sling that he had placed against his chest. Realizing that his *schweschder* didn't have a natural way with the *boppli*, Adam had done the best that he knew how by taking the infant out into the field with him.

71

Looking down at David's sleeping face, Adam felt like his heart was going to break. This wasn't how he had hoped things would go. Only a few short hours ago, he had expected a future with a loving *fraa* who would help to raise this *kinner*. Now, everything felt so uncertain. All the pain from Suzanna's earlier confession seemed to weigh on Adam like a ton of bricks.

"I wish I'd never met her, Lord," Adam said a quick prayer, admitting what was bothering him so much. "Suzanna only brought me pain."

The sound of approaching horses made him look up, and Adam saw the bishop's buggy pulling into their driveway. It appeared that he had made the trip with Sarah at his side. Not used to a visit from Amos, Adam wiped his dusty hands against his black pants and then started toward his home. He couldn't even begin to guess why Amos had made the trip.

"Afternoon, Adam," Amos said as he climbed down from his buggy seat and then reached up to offer his *fraa* a hand. As he reached their side, Adam was working on getting David out of the homemade sling. Glancing toward the front door, he saw that Barbara had stepped out on the porch and was leaning over the railing.

"I see you've got *boppli* David," Sarah said while giving a gentle smile in Adam's direction. "I'm sure that it's been a difficult day without Suzanna here to help."

Her words caused Adam to flinch and suck in a deep breath. "How did you know?"

Before Sarah could explain, Amos spoke up to say, "Let's go inside and talk for a little while."

Following the bishop and his *fraa* into the house, Adam wasn't sure that he wanted to hear whatever they had to say. He only wanted to forget about the young woman who had hurt him so deeply, and yet he longed for any news about where she had gone.

"Suzanna left this morning." It was Barbara who began the conversation, her words firm and cold as she passed out some glasses of freshly squeezed lemonade.

Amos took in a deep breath and gave a nod, his brow wrinkling as he looked down into his lemonade. "We know about what happened with Suzanna. She's the reason that Sarah and I decided to make a trip over here."

Letting his gaze travel to the bishop's *fraa*, Adam found himself holding his breath, anxious to hear any word about the woman who had deceived him and broken his heart. Glancing at his *schweschder,* he could see that Barbara was bristling, her hands clasping tighter against the clear glass she had been using.

"We found Suzanna on our back porch crying this morning," Sarah said, her brown eyes filling with sadness as she shook her head. The words instantly made Adam feel bad. He wanted to be angry at Suzanna and yet knowing that she had been crying made him want to go comfort her.

"Suzanna has made many mistakes," The bishop said as he folded his large hands together on the table. "But she confessed them all to us. Perhaps it's time that we offered her a little bit of *Gott's* grace. We must remember that the Lord always gives forgiveness to us when we hurt him... can't we offer the same to this poor, lost girl?"

Swallowing hard, Adam tried to get his emotions in check. Looking down at *boppli* David, who was sleeping in his arms, he found himself grappling with the feelings that threatened to overtake him.

"We had wondered if Suzanna wasn't somehow connected to little David from the start," Sarah said.

Her words made both Adam and Barbara sit up straighter and look at each other in surprise. Rushing to continue, Sarah said, "It just appeared likely since she and David appeared at the same time... and they seemed to have such a gut connection. We thought maybe *Gott* had brought her here for a reason." Her eyes looked up to meet Adam's. "And it seemed like she might have had a gut connection with you, as well."

"It was *gut* to see some joy in your sad eyes again," Amos said. "We hadn't seen it since Rosy passed away. We were praying that the Lord was going to give both you and Suzanna a fresh start."

Trying to glance away from their expectant stares, Adam worried that his guests would see the tears that were gathering in his eyes.

"This doesn't change anything!" Barbara said, her voice sounding harsh as she rose from her seat and began to gather the empty glasses. She worked frantically as if she had to do something, and cleaning was her only option. "That... that... woman still tricked us! She came into our lives, obviously with the intention of deceiving us all. She just wanted to secure a home for herself and her *boppli*. She set it all up so that she could just get close to Adam and make him believe that she loved him."

While these were all accusations that had been turning in Adam's mind throughout the morning, he found himself shaking his head. "It's not true, *schweschder*. When she first moved here, she thought that we were a married couple. I was the one that tried to get close to her... and she scolded me for being unfaithful to you."

"We believe that Suzanna honestly wants what is best for David," Sarah said. "If it had all been a trick, wouldn't she have taken him with her when she left this time?"

Barbara stood frozen in place, her mind obviously working as she tried to sort truth from lies. Slowly, her expression softened, and she let her body sink back down into her seat. "I suppose that is true."

With his *schweschder* silenced, Adam turned his full attention to the bishop when the wise older man began to speak to him.

"Adam, this is an issue of the heart, and I don't want to tell you what to do. I can't make you trust Suzanna again or regain what you've lost, but I can urge you to offer her some forgiveness. The poor girl is hurting, and she needs to know that she still has friends. We're afraid of what might happen with her if she leaves Faith's Creek right now."

The truth of Amos' words hit Adam like a ton of bricks. Where would Suzanna go if she left their community? Would she try to join another Amish district, or would she have to leave the faith behind completely?

Rising to his feet, Adam took a deep breath of air and swallowed hard. "I want to see her," he said. "I need to go talk to her."

As the Bishop and Sarah prepared to drive Adam home with them, he could only hope that Suzanna would still be there waiting.

CHAPTER TEN

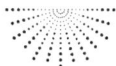

Jesus looked at them and said, "With man this is impossible, but with God all things are possible."
Matthew 19:26

S tanding in the guest bedroom of the Beiler's home, Suzanna stared out the window and allowed her gaze to travel across the lush, green fields outside the bishop's backyard. She had certainly destroyed everything gut... once again.

Shaking her head, she reached up to wipe at her

eyes. Although Sarah had instructed her to rest, Suzanna felt like all she could do was think and cry.

"How have I messed things up so badly, Lord?" she asked into the stillness of the room. She had prayed for *Gott* to forgive her, but it felt like she would never be able to forgive herself. She had hurt Adam deeply and even betrayed the trust of Barbara.

Looking down at her hands, Suzanna wrung them together and tried to consider her options. She couldn't stay here at Faith's Creek. Not after all that had happened. It was time for her to move on. She only hoped that Adam would continue to love David as his own and that he didn't resent the *boppli* for her mistakes.

"It's time to leave," she said the words to herself, the truth hitting her hard. She would need to hurry if she was going to make her escape before Amos and Sarah returned home.

The sound of the front door opening made her jump. It seemed like she had waited too long to leave. Glancing around the room, she wondered if she could try to sneak out before they tried to stop her.

"Suzanna!"

The voice made her stop cold in her tracks. Surely, her ears were playing tricks on her. Before Suzanna could even catch her breath, Adam's familiar form appeared in the bedroom doorway. He had David clasped in his arms, holding the boy tightly against his chest.

"Suzanna," Adam said, his voice catching in his throat as he looked at her, "I was afraid that... I worried that you might not be here anymore."

Giving a nod, Suzanna admitted that he was right. "I was actually just thinking about leaving." She couldn't even look him in the eyes, she had to look down at the hardwood floor and fight the tears that were about to overtake her.

"Where will you go next?" Adam asked, his voice husky.

Giving a shrug, Suzanna turned back toward the window. "I don't know. I just know that I need to get away from here. I need to leave Faith's Creek behind. The only way for David to have a gut life is if I'm not a part of it." She felt so overwhelmed with an urge to escape that she had to fight herself to hold her ground. Before she left, she had to let Adam know how sorry she was. Forcing herself to look at him, she said, "I am truly sorry, Adam. I had let myself believe that I could hide my past from everyone, but it seems to follow me wherever I go."

To her surprise, Adam's eyes were no longer condemning. Instead, they seemed to hold more softness than ever. Looking down at her son, Suzanna fought the urge to reach out and touch his soft cheek. "If things were different, then I truly would have loved to be your *fraa*. If I hadn't made so many mistakes in the past, perhaps I would be worthy of you. Now, if you excuse me, I need to get ready to go."

Suzanna made a step toward the door, but Adam reached out and grabbed her hand. She felt her heart give a leap as his rough skin touched hers.

"Why did you leave David?" Adam asked. His voice was husky, and it sounded like he might be battling tears himself. "When Barbara revealed your true identity, why didn't you take him with you?"

Her heart felt like it would break in two as her gaze

traveled from the man that she loved to the precious boy held in his arms. "I want the best for my son... and I am not the best. I knew that leaving him with you all would provide him with a *gut* life."

Adam was silent for a moment as if he was trying to wrap his mind around her words. Finally, he grabbed tighter to her hand. "Suzanna, I am not the best. I do love David like he is my own, and I will be a gut *daed* to him, but he needs so much more than I can offer. He needs his *mamm*." Rushing to continue, Adam said, "If I was the *gut* man you think I am, I would have never let you go. When you left this morning, I was so caught up in my own emotions that I allowed my pain to direct me. I should have followed you when you tried to leave. I should have forced you to tell me the rest of your story."

Reaching up to wipe at her eyes, Suzanna felt like she couldn't handle the emotions that were assailing her. Tears ran down Adam's cheeks, and she had to battle the urge to reach out and comfort him.

"Suzanna," Adam said, "We have all made mistakes, and the Lord offers us all forgiveness. The things that you have done wrong in the past do not keep you from being a *gut* woman. You are a wonderful *mamm*... and you're the woman that I love and want in my life. You are the one that I want to marry, no matter what mistakes you may have made in the past. I still love you!"

The words he spoke seemed too gut to even be true. How could he still love her after all that she had done and the ways that she had deceived him?

Adam rearranged David in his arms and passed the *boppli* to her. Taking the sleeping kinner against her body, Suzanna felt tears of joy run down her cheeks as she looked into his precious face.

Grabbing her by the shoulders, Adam pulled her closer to him and stared down into her eyes with a gaze that was full of genuine love. Lifting her chin with his thumb, he whispered, "I can't picture my life without you, Suzanna. Please, do me the honor of being my *fraa*."

Realizing that Adam still cared for her despite her mistakes, Suzanna felt her heart surge with joy. Reaching out, she wrapped an arm around his waist and let him pull her into a hug.

"Of course, Adam Wengerd," she said, her voice

choking up with each word that she said. "I will marry you. Thank *Gott*! I will marry you!"

Holding each other, the couple were overwhelmed with the promise of a fresh start and a beautiful life that would be shared side-by-side.

CHAPTER ELEVEN

~

For everything that was written in the past was
written to teach us, so that through the endurance
taught in the Scriptures and the encouragement they
provide we might have hope.
Romans 15:4

~

Saying goodbye to the last of the guests, Suzanna watched as her new husband, Adam, walked them out to their waiting buggy. It was hard to believe that it had been six months since the dear man had asked her to be his *fraa*. Now, she had finally been able to stand before the entire Amish community and promise before *Gott* to love Adam Wengerd for the rest of their lives together.

"I put David down to bed."

The voice of Barbara made Suzanna jump, and she turned on her heel to see Adam's *schweschder* staring at her, a look of uncertainty in her eyes. The other woman began to shuffle her feet before saying, "I supposed that the newlyweds might like to spend a little time alone together at least tonight."

Suzanna felt a twinge of red come to her cheeks as she nodded her head. "*Denke*, Barbara."

As was the typical Amish custom, there would be no honeymoon after the barnyard wedding there at the Wengerd home. Instead, the new couple would simply start on their new lives together by following their usual routine.

Turning back to the window, Suzanna anxiously waited for Adam to return to her side. After such a wonderful day, she hated to be apart from him for even a few minutes.

"Suzanna," Barbara's voice caught her attention, and she turned back around. "I really do appreciate the fact that you and Adam are going to let me continue to live here."

Smiling, Suzanna gave a shrug. "We wouldn't have it any other way! We wouldn't know what to do without you here with us. I think David has even gotten pretty used to spending time with his auntie."

The silence in the room was uncomfortable. Although Barbara had not caused any trouble since the day that Adam proposed to Suzanna for the second time, there always seemed to be a tension between the two women. Suzanna couldn't shake the feeling that her new *schweschder-in-law* didn't like her.

"I'm glad your parents could come to the wedding." It seemed like Barbara was trying to make small talk now.

Reaching up to run her finger across the cool glass of the window, Suzanna nodded her head. *Ach,* she was certainly glad to! After all that had happened between her and her family, she had worried that they would never want to see her again. But, as it turned out, *Gott* had a plan to restore their relationship as well. Despite all the mistakes that Suzanna had made in the past, the Lord was faithful and was constantly proving that she truly was forgiven for her bad choices. It would be so gut that David could know his entire family.

"Suzanna," Barbara spoke her name again, and this time, she stepped forward. "I am not very gut about saying things, but I feel like I have to. All those months back when I revealed your secrets to Adam, it was wrong of me. I now know that. I should have come to you first rather than telling him about your past. I was just so upset and was trying to protect him."

Seeing that tears were starting to gather in Barbara's eyes, Suzanna reached out and put a reassuring hand on her shoulder. "It's all right! I do understand..."

Barbara didn't wait on her to finish before she said, "When I was watching the wedding today, I noticed how happy Adam looked beside you. If things had gone the way I wanted, he never would have had a chance to experience that happiness. I hope you don't hold any anger against me because of what I did and how harsh I was to you."

"Barbara," Suzanna said her name softly and let out a laugh, "I don't hold it against you at all! We have all made mistakes and poor decisions. Thankfully, *Gott* is gracious and works through our silly choices. I know that you were only trying to protect your *bruder,* and I love you for caring about him so much. I want you to be a part of our lives. I have already seen how much David is warming up to you, and I can tell that you are going to be the best aunt for him. I hope that you and I can eventually become friends."

Tears began to pour down Barbara's face, and, in an uncharacteristic move, she stepped forward and pulled Suzanna into a hug. "I want to be more than friends, Suzanna, dear! I want the two of us to become *schweschders.*"

Suzanna couldn't hide the smile on her face as she felt the warmth of the other woman's embrace. The ability to share a relationship with Adam's harsh older *schweschder* was something that she had only dreamed could be possible.

The door swung open, and Adam stepped inside the house, the sound of his boots hitting the hardwood floor and alerting the two women that he was there.

Looking up at him, both Suzanna and Barbara had tear-filled eyes. Instant surprise covered Adam's face, but it was quickly replaced by pure joy. Making his way across the room, he put a hand on each of their shoulders' and smiled broadly. "The two women I love most in the world are finally getting along! This has to truly be a miracle."

Letting loose of Barbara, Suzanna wrapped her arms around her new husband and leaned her head against his shoulder. "*Jah* – we've certainly been blessed with a large share of miracles!"

CHAPTER TWELVE

28 And we know that in all things God works for the good of those who love him, who have been called according to his purpose.
Romans 8:28

Standing on the front porch of the Wengerd home, Suzanna looked out across the lush farmland. In the distance, she could see Adam working in the fields, plowing the ground so that it would be ready for the crops that he was preparing to plant.

Grasping the glass of home-squeezed lemonade tighter in her hand, she smiled to herself as she started down the porch steps and toward her husband.

Making her way across the soft turf, she relished the warm day, enjoying every sight that spring had to offer. Traveling without her shoes, the blades of soft grass tickled her bare feet. In some ways, it seemed like just yesterday when she had discovered this farm and thought it was the right place to leave David while, in others, it felt like a lifetime.

"Hello there," she called out to her husband when she reached the edge of the plowed ground.

Looking up in surprise, Adam stopped the horse, his face breaking out in a grin when he saw his *fraa*. Tying the horse's rein's so they couldn't move, he walked to meet her.

"I thought you might need something cool on this warm day," Suzanna said as she passed the lemonade in his direction. Smiling even wider, Adam tipped the glass up and chugged the lemonade in one swallow.

Raising her eyebrows, Suzanna said, "Looks like I was right, you were thirsty."

"Looks like you make gut lemonade!" he returned with a boyish smile. Reaching out, he pulled her into a hug, bringing her body tightly against his. Lowering his voice, he said, "Your lemonade is even better than Barbara's now... just don't tell her I said that!"

Giving her husband a playful slap, Suzanna giggled. "Your *schweschder* is still the best cook, hands down! But I'm glad for that." Nodding her head toward a nearby tree, she directed her husband to look where his *schweschder* was sitting on a bench with David curled up on her lap. Now more than a year old, David loved to spend time with his Aunt Barb.

"It looks like she's reading him a story," Adam said as he leaned his head against the top of Suzanna's. "I'm so happy that they get along."

"I'm happy about everything." Tears threatened to overtake her as Suzanna considered all that had happened since she arrived at Faith's Creek. She had been given the opportunity to not only get a fresh start but also a loving family and a renewed faith.

What would have happened to her if *Gott* had not directed her to this sweet Amish district?

Glancing up at her husband, Suzanna asked, "Do you ever think about my past and the bad choices that I've made?" She had found herself gathering the courage to ask what bothered her the most, "Do you ever regret that I had a *boppli* with another man... and that I had such a wild start?"

Turning Suzanna in his arms so that he could look at her, Adam's expression reflected his gentle, pure heart. "No, not at all. While I wish that you hadn't gone through so much, *Gott* has worked it all out for our gut. The past is in the past, and I spend my time looking forward to the future." Reaching out a gentle finger, he stroked it against Suzanna's cheek. "And I believe that we will have the best future together."

Putting an arm around his waist, Suzanna considered the best way to tell him her exciting news. Looking down at her bare feet, she wiggled her toes in the grass and grinned to herself, "*Jah* – we will have a gut future on the farm here with Barbara and David... and our new *boppli*."

When Adam didn't speak instantly, Suzanna had to

look up at him just to see if he had caught her meaning. Her sweet husband was simply staring at her, his jaw dropped open in surprise. "Do you mean...?" his voice trailed off and left Suzanna to nod her head.

She placed a hand on her abdomen and smiled softly. "That's right. By this fall, we should have a sweet little *bruder* or *schweschder* for David to enjoy."

Unable to contain his excitement, Adam let out a *yeehaw* before clasping her even tighter against his body. As he talked about the upcoming *boppli*, Suzanna leaned her head against his strong chest and soaked in the warmth of her surroundings.

Despite the mistakes that she had made, *Gott* truly had been gut to her. He had continued to look out for her and take care of her even when she was lost in the midst of her mistakes. Now, Suzanna didn't think she could ever be thankful enough for the many blessings that had been poured on her life! She and Adam truly would enjoy a blessed future!

Emma King hitched up faithful old Dusty to the buggy. The big, bay horse had been a present from her *Daed* when she first ventured out on her now flourishing baking business. With a sigh, she realized that it had been three years ago now. Three happy... but long years, three years where nothing had changed... Shaking away her sad thoughts, she hummed a hymn as she returned to the house and soon exited with a box of freshly baked fruit pies. There were all sorts, all homemade by her, and all her own special recipe. This batch included apple, strawberry, and wild berries. Her *Mamm*, Nancy King, followed closely behind with another box, this one of pecan pies. She had a light coat draped over her arm.

As they loaded the pies into the buggy, Emma felt her mind begin to wander. *What else can I do with my life?* Emma often asked herself this. *I could be baking for my husband and kinner,* she sighed. This thought frequently crossed her mind whenever she set about baking her pies—which was almost every day now. *I guess I have to resign myself to a life destined to be that of an old maid. Twenty-two and unmarried and not a prospect in sight,* she sighed again.

"Are you sure you want to deliver those pies now," her *Mamm* asked. "You've been up just about all night getting everything ready. That sigh you just let out sounds awfully tired to me."

Emma smiled her sweet smile. "*Denke.* But I'm all right. I'll hop in bed as soon as I return. It won't take me long, and the customers will be waiting." Emma hated to let anyone down.

Amber, Emma's younger sister, skipped out behind them with her satchel tucked under her arm. At eight years old, she looked so cute with her blonde hair tucked beneath her *kapp* and her blue eyes all bright and eager. Emma's two brothers, twelve-year-old John, and fifteen-year-old Joseph, had gotten up earlier with *Daed* and had already taken care of the morning chores. It was always a rush. Feeding and milking the cows, collecting the eggs from the hens, after that, they all enjoyed breakfast together, then the boys had left for school. Amber, as always, was pushing it to the last minute. Emma smiled, she was grateful to the two boys for their help in bringing in the milk, butter, and eggs for her, but she had a soft spot for Amber, and she indicated the buggy.

With a grin, Amber climbed on board, it would be much quicker if Emma dropped her off, and she knew her sister would always do it.

"It's overcast, so you may need your coat," *Mamm* said, as she placed the box next to the others in the buggy and popped the coat on top of it. Emma secured the boxes so they would not slide as she traveled over the gravel roads. She climbed up next to Amber, who was already licking on a candied apple.

"*Jah. Denke.* Bye, *Mamm.* I'll be gone all day as I have to stop into town to drop off ten of the pies at the Soup Shop. I may stop by and visit with Lydia for a short while. Do you need me to bring you anything back?"

"*Nee*. Nothing at all. Drive carefully. Amber, you be good in school and put that candied apple away until lunchtime," *Mamm* King said.

"I will, *Mamm*. Bye." Amber took a couple more licks before re-wrapping the apple in the wax paper.

Emma's dark brown hair was tucked neatly beneath her kapp, the tendrils that escaped offsetting her gray eyes. She was not what one would call beautiful, but she was fair to look upon. Emma had only one flaw—a flaw that in her mind was a major setback to her moving forward with the one thing that she thought was missing from her life... she was overweight, and no one wanted to court her.

"Emma, may I please spend the day with you and help you make your deliveries? You do look tired," Amber said. "I'm already ahead in school, so I won't miss much."

"Sorry, but you cannot miss school. Turn right, Dusty," Emma said, giving a slight tug to the reins. Emma made a few deliveries before dropping Amber off at the schoolhouse. John and Joseph were waiting for them. As she was pulling off, she heard someone yell, "Hey, fatso!" This comment was followed by laughter. Emma smiled for the sake of her siblings, but the comment cut her deep inside. Ignoring the hurt, she waved a cheerful goodbye to them. "Be good. I'll have a pie waiting for you when you come home. I love you."

She straightened her back, clicked at Dusty, and set out to finish her deliveries. After delivering her last ten pies to the Soup Shop in town, Emma sat at a small table by the window to sip on a bowl of potato soup, embellished with bacon, before heading home. She casually glanced around. There was an elderly couple having tea and cake. A mother and her two daughters were having a late lunch meal of sandwiches and soup. Two men were enjoying coffee. Everyone was with someone, everyone had a family... only Emma was all alone.

A nice-looking young man entered the shop, his eyes met hers as he randomly glanced over the room. He took a couple steps in her direction. Emma's heart started to flutter as she lowered her eyes to her bowl of soup. She felt disappointed when he walked passed her to the back of the shop. She left her half-eaten bowl of soup and hurried out of the Soup Shop. *I'm like a fly on the wall, no one ever notices me,* she thought as she climbed into her buggy and headed on home. *Gott, what is wrong with me! It seems everyone has someone they can share with except me. But who would want a twenty-two-year-old fatso?* Sadness crept over her and stayed with her all the way home.

She fought the temptation to drive straight past her best friend Lydia's house. It would be easier to just go home, but she had promised her she would stop by. Being a person of her word, she forced on her happy face as she knocked on Lydia's front door. Lydia had always been an encouragement to her even when she was not trying to be.

Soon she was drinking strong, black coffee with her friend as they nibbled on one of her special pies. This one was strawberry, and it was melt in the mouth delicious. Tasting of summer and all its promises.

"You deserve *Mamm* of the Year Award," Emma said to Lydia. "I just don't see how you can juggle a twenty-month-old, housework, do your gardening, and all expecting your second child any moment now, and still move with as much energy as you do. I guess some women just have a knack for motherhood."

"Are you saying you don't?" Lydia asked.

Emma shrugged, but said pleasantly, "I'm still unmarried. No beau in sight for miles to come."

"Just keep living your life the way *Gott* intended. The right *mann* will come along. He is out there, he just hasn't tasted one of your pies yet. When he does, he'll come running and panting after you and beg you to never leave him," Lydia said with a laugh.

Emma joined in the laughter, but she felt empty inside. Empty, and so alone.

"You seem to be taking it well, though," Lydia said.

If you only knew how much I am hurting on the inside, Emma thought. "*Jah.* What else can I do but to take it well?" Emma swallowed hard, knowing she was not being completely truthful.

"You know the Bible says to trust in *Gott* with all your heart and lean not unto your own understanding and He will direct your path and will grant you the desires of your heart. Good things come to those who wait," Lydia said. "Who says you have to be married by a certain age, anyway?"

"*Jah.* Who says?"

The friends enjoyed a slice of Emma's creamy strawberry pie as they conversed more.

A little girl clung onto Emma's legs as if she would never let go. In her throat, she was making small noises that were almost like crying, yet Lydia took no notice.

"Sandy seems a little whiny," Emma said, changing the subject as she stroked the child's head. "Do you want me to take her outside for a while?"

"Ignore her. She's been like that lately. *Grossmammi* says when they're that age, they tend to cling more to you when you're expecting another child. I guess she thinks I'm going to love her less," Lydia said with a laugh.

"Like I said, you deserve *Mamm* of the Year Award," Emma said. "I don't know if I could juggle that many hats at one time."

"Ach. *Gott* will give you the grace to handle anything," Lydia said.

Emma nodded, and they talked quietly for a while.

∽

Instead of heading straight for home after her visit with Lydia, Emma decided to go by the creek. It was her favorite place for conversing with *Gott* whenever she was troubled. She had been stopping there a lot lately as no one seemed to understand what she was going through. Besides, she did not want to burden others with her worries. What good would it do? People had their own troubles to deal with, so Emma kept hers to herself.

Pulling Dusty up, she loosened his reins so that he could graze on the lush grass while she sat for a while. It was so nice by the creek at that time of the day, just before the children came out of school was the quietest time. The birds seem to be taking a rest from singing all day. Even the insects seem to be taking a break from hopping and flying and zinging about. 'Come, take a rest and lay your burdens by my bank,' the creek seemed to say, as it provided a quiet respite for all who would accept the invitation.

Gott will give you the grace to handle anything, kept running through her head.

"*Gott*," she prayed. "It seems You made me different. I'm twenty-two and not married. All my friends are married and are living their lives. What am I doing with mine? Making pies. Is this what I have to resign myself to doing for the rest of my life? What's wrong with me? You made women to marry, to keep house, to bear children. I know I can be a good wife... so how come you have not given me a husband? Is there one out there for me?"

As she poured out her heart to God, the tears quietly trickled down, and she was lost in her thoughts and her sorrow.

A chuckle caused her to turn around. Some children were standing partially hidden behind the trees with mischievous grins on their faces. Emma had not heard them approach the creek.

"Hey, it's fatso!" one of them shouted. "Let's have some fun."

"You're as big as a house," someone said in a sing-song voice. "Where's the front door?"

"My brother says he would never marry you because you're too fat."

"Amber's sister is F-A-T. She needs to push away from the table more."

Emma turned away, but she could not stop the tears. Children could be so mean.

You can read these 15 delightful Amish romances for FREE with Kindle Unlimited Grab 15 Tales of Amish Love and Grace now

All my books are FREE on Kindle Unlimited

If you love Amish Romance, the sweet, clean stories of
Sarah Miller you can join me for the latest news on
upcoming books http://eepurl.com/bdEdSn

These are some of my reader favorites:

A Spring Baby Dilemma

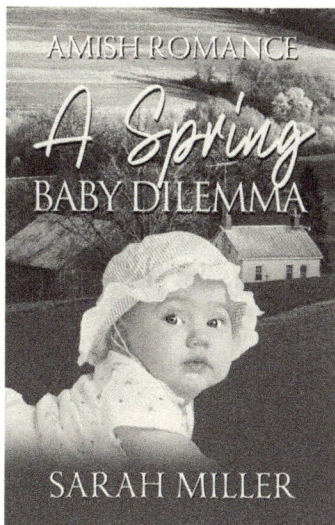

The Amish Healer Box Set

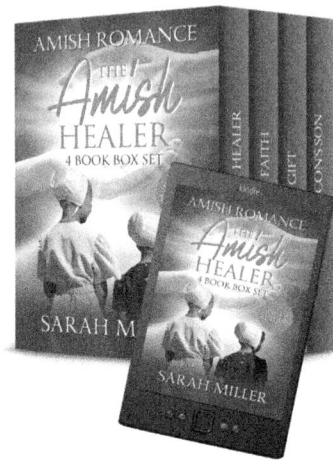

Find all Sarah's books on Amazon and click the yellow follow button

This book is dedicated to the wonderful Amish people and the faithful life that they live.

Go in peace my friends.

As an independent author, Sarah relies on your support. If you enjoyed this book, please leave a review on Amazon or Goodreads.

ABOUT THE AUTHOR

Sarah Miller was born in Pennsylvania and spent her childhood close to the Amish people. Weekends were spent doing chores; quilting or eventually babysitting in the community. She grew up to love their culture and the simple lifestyle and had many Amish friends. The one thing that you can guarantee when you are near the Amish, Sarah believes is that you will feel close to God.

Many years later she married Martin who is the love of her life and moved to England. There she started to write stories about the Amish. Recently after a lot of persuasion from her best friend she has decided to publish her stories. They draw on inspiration from her relationship with the Amish and with God and she hopes you enjoy reading them as much as she did writing them. Many of the stories are based on true events but names have been changed and even though they are authentic at times artistic license has been used.

Sarah likes her stories simple and to hold a message and they help bring her closer to her faith. She currently lives in Yorkshire, England with her husband Martin and seven very spoiled chickens.

She would love to meet you on facebook at https://www.facebook.com/SarahMillerBooks

Sarah hopes her stories will both entertain and inspire and she wishes that you go with God.

Made in the USA
Las Vegas, NV
21 August 2021